CHILDRENZ ONE.

Stories for 8-11 year olds.

Selected and edited

by

Jill Darragh

Rangitawa
PUBLISHING

Childrenz One first published 2014.

Published by Rangitawa Publishing, Feilding, New Zealand.

www.rangitawapublishing.com

rangitawa@xtra.co.nz

ISBN 978-0-9941088-1-4

<u>From the Editor</u>

This is a selection of stories from the entrants of the Rangitawa Publishing 'Write a Children's Story' competition 2014.

Childrenz One is a collection of the entries suitable for readers of 8-11 years old. **Childrenz Two** comprises of stories for young adult readers.

The writer's ages range from eight years old to adult. I would like to thank all the authors who supported this project.

Please note that all due care has been taken to ensure there are no errors in this book but if readers find a mistake they are welcome to contact me and I will correct the file for future readers.

Jill Darragh 2014.

Contents

At the Beach

By Kezia Rogers age 10. (1st)

Cassie was bored. All games had been played, all books had been read, and all DVDs had been watched. Her brother, Charlie, and Dad were at a rugby game in Wellington, and there was just her and Mum. Then she thought of a great idea.

"Mum, can I please go down to the beach for a bit? I'll be back for dinner".

"Sure, but take a jacket".

Cassie pulled on her All Blacks jandals, grabbed her blue jacket and walked out of the house. Down the driveway she went until she came to the gate. She opened it, and stepped out onto the grass.

Cassie walked down the road. She passed many houses, and many more trees. Eventually she came to the bridge. She walked over it and stared at the shimmering water of the river below. She heard a splash, and wondered if it was a mermaid. Continuing on her way she stepped off the bridge into the pine forest. Then she turned and ran towards the sea.

She charged across the huge flat area not stopping for anyone or anything. Now she was staggering up the steep dune, climbing, climbing. Cassie scrambled up the last part and stood, staring at the sea. The waves slapped and slid like broken glass. She tasted salt.

Laughing happily, she skipped down the other side. Then she frowned. It was low tide, so she'd have to run all the way down. Cassie started running. She sprinted across the damp sand like a wild horse. Her feet pounded on the beach. Occasionally she would step on a shell but Cassie kept running. She was almost at the ocean now! Her legs were yelling at her "Stop! We're too tired to go any further", but she ignored her body, sprinting and leaping over the piles of driftwood. Finally she halted. She was at the sea.

Dipping her toes in the icy water she murmured, "Oh, so cold".

Her feet were freezing so she jumped out of the waves and tore up the beach to the high tide mark. She tiptoed along the sand, not wanting to disturb the wildlife, if there was any. Then she saw it. A long brown length of wood, with a hole on a fat bit looking like a head with an eye. It was a driftwood snake! She picked it up and looked around. Cassie couldn't see another beach creature, but what was that over there? She ran over to it and found a gigantic horse mussel, silvery, shiny. She poked a hole in it for an eye and exclaimed "Now it's a fish!"

She dragged them after her to a pile of sand decorated with shells. She noticed that it wasn't a pile of sand, but a sculptured crocodile. It had a fence of spikes along its back. She left the crocodile for the sea to chew away, but wished she could take the other creatures home. She knew what Mum would say though – "Get that wood and the shell out of the house now!"

No, it would be better to leave them here. Cassie walked down until the waves lapped at her toes. She hurled the fish into the sea where it sank to the bottom, resting on the seabed. Then it was the snake's turn and it floated, winking as if to say "Thank you".

Cassie took up a large pearly pink shell and stuck it in her pocket. Then she went home the way she had come. When she was finally back at the beach house, she pressed the shell to her ear, and heard the sound of the sea.

An Unlikely Hero

By Alex Wood age 11. (2nd)

The farm expanded into view as they drew near. Bentley's owner was going on a holiday, so he was being dropped off at his cousin's farm.

"Goodbye my little Puppykins. See you soon!.

The car door slammed shut and she was gone in a cloud of powdery dust that covered Bentley's well groomed fur.

Bentley turned to meet his cousins Tahi, Rua, Toru and Wha. "Come on Bentley we're going sheep hopping."

They led Bentley to a fence, slithered under the gap underneath and out the other side. Tahi jumped over one of the sheep and into a mud puddle. Rua, Toru and Wha followed. Bentley crawled on his belly and tried to squeeze under the fence. He didn't move. He tried again. He couldn't budge. He was stuck. It must be the organic chocolate flavoured doggie biscuits he snacked on. He should really go on a diet he thought. Bentley managed to slither backwards and out the way he came.

"Well we're going to have fun anyway" said Rua with a sneer, and they ran off.

Bentley walked towards the farmhouse and sat down in the long grass. How am I going to last a week here? he thought. His once beautifully groomed fur was full of burrs and dried mud and he didn't smell of rose scented doggy shampoo anymore.

CLASH! CLASH!

"Dinner" hollered the farmer. Bentley's ears perked up and he raced inside the farm house expectantly. But where were the shiny metal bowls with his name engraved? Where was Mrs Newman's Organic Pet Chow? The farmer threw a greasy slab of dog roll on the floor. The other dogs were on top of it at once, fighting over every scrap. "Squelch!" A mushy pile of mashed potato landed inches from Bentley. He sniffed it. YUCK. I'd best just go to bed he thought.

Bentley followed the sound of snoring. It led to a large kennel with its fading paint flaking off. No embroidered cushions and fluffy blankets here! He sat down on the hard dirt floor, his tummy empty.

"I miss my home!" He whimpered. Poor Bentley, little did he know, things were about to change.

Bentley woke up and for a second he forgot where he was. Then it all came flooding back. He sighed and stretched his sore, stiff limbs. He watched his cousins scavenge the last scraps of the farmer's breakfast off the floor. Without another word they walked out the door

"Hey" Bentley called. "Where are you going?"

"*We're* rounding up sheep," said Toru. And *you* can't come because *you're* useless."

Without another word they turned and stalked past him.

Poor Bentley, he ran until he could run no more. He collapsed onto the grass. Tears rolled down his fur. He was just a useless, pampered city dog. He just wanted to go home.

Suddenly he stopped crying and cocked his ears. What was that noise? Feeble cries sounded not far away. He followed the calls to a large mud pool. There was the farmer's quad bike and the cries seemed to be coming from underneath it! Bentley looked under the bike. There was the farmer's son Sam! Sam was sinking further and further into the mud pool even as he watched.

Bentley's owner took him for swims daily because she believed it was nutritious for his coat, so he was a very strong swimmer. He jumped in and grabbed Sam's checkered shirt with his teeth, paddling to the bank with all his doggy might. The pair of them lay gasping on the bank.

"Chuggachuggachugga".

Bentley's long hair and floppy ears were blown back as a large red shape came hovering into view. It was the Westpac Rescue helicopter!

Sam was rolled onto a stretcher and moved onto the helicopter. The paramedic patted Bentley's head.

"You've done a great job," she whispered. 'We'll take over from here," and the helicopter flew up and away on its journey to Starship Hospital.

"Thank goodness you found him, because we are not very strong swimmers," said Rua. Bentley smiled with pride. Maybe being a pampered city dog wasn't such a bad thing after all.

<u>Shadowfang Returns</u>

By Benjamin Limsowtin age 11 (3rd)

     "In the castle Ekron lives a population of 700,000 men and women, a lot for one castle to hold. We are in the year 3062 and the current King is Peter; he assures us there is no danger there…" The teacher seemed to drone on forever.

     "Oh my God be quiet!" Leon whispered to Jack, his friend.

     "I can't believe we're *here* for a class trip!"

     "It's better than being in school though," Jack whispered back

"True that. Oh we're landing," replied Leon And so they were. The massive purple bus with the school logo on it flashed across the castle grounds. Leon and his friend Jack would have been bored to death, had it not been for the dragon.

They were busy staring at an osmium suit of armour when Peter, King of Ekron, walked in. They all bowed low (girls did curtsies).

"Good afternoon your majesty," whispered the teacher to the King's grim looking face.

"I don't have time for this. Shadowfang the dragon has returned. I need you and your class to evacuate this castle immediately," said the King. A few people remained motionless.

"Who *is* Shadowfang anyway?" asked someone.

"He is a black dragon who, when he arrived, tore down many villages and castles until we chased him away. Now you need to go!!" snapped the King. The teacher led all the students from the armoury, not realising that Jack and Leon lingered behind.

"You want to see the dragon?" asked Leon to Jack, who grinned and said "Yeah you got a plan?"

When everyone left the armoury, Leon looked around "Coast is clear" he whispered.

At first things were going well when they heard a *CRASH* on the roof above them.

"RUN!!" Jack yelled as he sprinted down to the bus. Leon however, stayed because he had not done all this for nothing! *He* wanted to see the dragon.

Leon crept out of the Armoury and was surprised to see over five hundred armed men in the hall. Luckily no one looked twice at him. 'Great!' he thought, and he followed the mass of men into the castle's highest tower. On the tower next to him he could see a giant black dragon that was flicking away gunmen as if they weren't there. He also saw a massive Eon cannon being pointed at the dragon's head.

"AIM…AIM…FIRE!" he heard the general (or so he presumed) yelling. They didn't need to be told twice, a thick yellow ray fired onto the dragons thick hide but it pinged off, just like when you throw a rubber ball on a wall.

Panic! Shock! Fear! That is what Leon felt at that moment. He noticed the King wearing the osmium armour that Leon had been looking at. He flew up to the intimidating beast and went for the mouth. Now, Leon had seen the king's sword before, but had never seen it being used. It was as sharp as diamond. He cut the lower lip of the dragon and cut the upper eye, before he was knocked down by that massive tail.

Leon had to do something, he knew that the weak point of a dragon was its stomach so he took one of the injured soldiers' Ion sword (Ion not Eon, big difference), put on the man's jetpack and flew up to battle. He went straight to the stomach and hacked at it with all his might, and eventually it tore, releasing a tidal wave of green blood.

When it finally ended, Leon was surrounded by cheers of victory from the Ekron soldiers. He flew down to the bus before anyone saw him. It was a long, long way to the bus so Jack had only just got there. When Leon was in his seat, Jack whispered to him "Lets never do that again, agreed?"

"I dunno, if you stayed with me you'd think differently" replied Leon.

"What do you mean?" asked Jack.

"Adventure!" replied Leon.

FISHING WITH FRANKIE AND JEMMA!!

By Carol Burrows

Jemma and Frankie ran helter skelter to the shed.

"Help me find the fishing lines. Come on Jemma, hurry up before Dad leaves without us!"

Frankie's ruddy cheeks spattered with freckles, his stub nose and fiery, spikey, red hair standing on end, was frantically throwing everything in the shed aside, searching for their fishing lines.

"Where are they? Help me Jemma, quick, quick, you know how impatient Dad gets. He'll take off in a minute."

"Keep your hair on Frankie. I remember we put them in that box when we tidied the shed."

"Cool, so we did and the knife and hooks are here too. Let's go."

Smartly they ran to the car, where Dad sat twiddling with the radio, trying to find the weather report. It was not often they went out with Dad alone, especially now he had separated from Mum.

Jemma had put on her daggiest jeans and her bright orange tee-shirt. She took an old sweat shirt in case it became cold and her beanie covered her blonde hair.

"Do you think we should take our jackets Dad in case it comes up rough?"

"She'll be right. Hope you've grabbed your gumboots, you'll need them. Jump in and we're away before the tide turns and the fish swim back to sea."

The old Datsun took off down the winding, shingle road to the West Coast.

"Did you bring the bait Dad?'

"Of course son and a bucket and a knife to gut the fish."

"How about something for us to eat?" Jemma piped up.

Dad laughed "First catch your fish Jemma and then we'll have it for lunch!"

The children looked at each other and groaned. It could be a long, hungry day, if they didn't get any bites.

Dad grinned, "All you two ever think of is your stomach," he laughed.

They travelled through dense bush to reach a spot where Dad had fished, when he was a boy. Soon they turned off the road onto a dirt track, where native ferns grew amongst the Matai trees and the occasional Ponga.

The branches of the trees formed a canopy in places and the dank smell of wet vegetation filled their nostrils. To the children's delight, several times they drove through muddy fords, before they reached the river.

Silence! Only the bird song and the symphony of the stream as it ran over the rocks, could be heard when they turned the engine off. The place was deserted, except for sand flies that descended on them, the moment they stepped out of the car.

"Here you two smother yourselves in this repellent or you'll be eaten alive." Dad said.

"Get a move on. Let's unpack the boot and get those lines set up. Frankie you carry the bait."

"Worms ooh goodie. Fish love these wiggly things, we should catch plenty!" Jemma chortled as she peered into the bucket. Frankie grabbed a handful and tried to put them down her neck.

"Dad! Dad! Help, Frankie's teasing me." She gave him a push.

"Now, come on both of you and get your lines ready, your making such a noise the fish will swim away. Jemma, bring me your line and I'll help you bait it."

Dad laboriously twisted the worm onto the hook, sticking his tongue out while he concentrated and looking so hilarious that Jemma stifled a giggle. Frankie gazed deeply into the water where he could see several very tiny fish swimming lazily around.

"Dad is there any gold in this river?"

"Perhaps there would've been long ago. Thousands of miners came to the coast to seek their fortune in the 1860"s. That's over one hundred years ago. See those piles of stones, they're the tailings left behind when they were gold panning."

"Did they get much around here?"

"Some made a fortune, but others went home broke."

"Golly, do you think we could find some?"

"Afraid its long gone mate. Those miners did it really tough here as there were no roads. They had to cut tracks through the bush to get to the river and had to live on wood pigeons, fern, Konini berries and any fish they could catch."

The children listened entranced and found it hard to imagine.

"There were no shops to buy from and many became very sick and died out here. There were fights too, over gold, and many murder; it wasn't a nice place to come for many."

"Sad too for families left behind," Frankie chimed in.

"Frankie, come on we came here to fish!"

Jemma's patience was wearing thin. She concentrated on the line she had left tied up and suddenly cried out, "Quick Dad I think there's something on it."

Sure enough the line was taught. It was really heavy too and Dad had difficulty pulling it in. Frankie dropped his line on the bank and came running over to help.

"Probably snagged on a rock," he said knowledgeably.

Dad disagreed. "Whatever it is it's trying to get away, but it's well and truly caught."

The children leaned as far over the bank as they dared. Suddenly Dad gave an almighty heave and an ugly head appeared.

"What is it? What is it?"

Jemma and Frankie leaped up and down with excitement.

"Hang on a minute and you'll see."

Dad was straining hard to get it on the bank. It was the ugliest fish the children had ever seen. They watched excitedly as it thrashed around and Dad tried to dislodge the hook from its mouth.

"It's an eel. They live under the banks and it must have been really hungry as it tried to eat that worm Jemma."

"Can we eat it?" Frankie thought of his stomach first.

"No, it's a mud eel."

"Yuk! Frankie you try to get it in the bucket. I'm not touching that ugly head." Jemma squirmed.

"Perhaps we should throw it back."

"Depends," Dad said. "Could be good tucker for the dog if we cut it up."

"I don't want it in the car. It looks like a Dragon. The skin is all slimy and wet."

"It can't hurt you Jemma. What do you think Frankie?"

He shuddered "I don't think Buster would like it if we took it home, neither would Mum"

"Right that settles it. Back it goes."

With that he threw it into the creek and they watched it swim away. Dad looked at his watch.

"Let's have some lunch now. Tie your lines to a branch while I open the picnic basket."

They spread an old blanket on the flattest spot they could see and grabbed a sandwich each, loving the delicious roast pork and apple sauce. There were muffins with blueberries and some apples too and a glass of coke each to wash it all down.

Dad had done well!

While they were eating their lunch Dad told them both tales of the Brown mud fish that lived in the rivers of the coast.

"You never know you might catch one of these."

"They can survive without water as long as it is in a damp place, with plenty of mud where they can curl up and hide. Sometimes they hide in the roots of trees. They can breathe through their skin and don't need to be in water to live but they are very ugly things, worse than the eel you caught Jemma.''

"Let's go and look for one after lunch Jemma." Frankie beamed.

"Yuk! Frankie, we would get very dirty."

"That's right Jemma. I had better not take you home covered in mud. Mum will be annoyed."

Satisfied, they lay back in the sunshine and it wasn't long before Dad dozed off. Frankie gave Jemma a nudge and putting his finger to his lips, beckoned for her to follow him. Quietly they made their way to the bank and followed until it reached a bend in the river.

"Where are we going?" Jemma queried. "I hope we aren't going to look for those Mud fish."

"Nah. Remember when I asked about the gold and Dad said they had taken some from here? When I was fishing I noticed a pile of shingle, just past this bend. It probably came from when the miners were exploring here and these are the remains of the tailings that they've already checked. I thought if we could get out to them, we could see if they missed any gold."

"But, but," Jemma gasped. "They look like a pile of old stones and they are right in the middle of the river."

"They are the tailings Dad was talking about. They're all that's left after they check the stones for gold. It's not far out to them though and the river isn't very deep here. Come on don't be a nerd."

Gingerly they entered the river and carefully waded out to where the tailings sat, probably undisturbed for many years. The water was very clear and only just below their knees. They began to scratch through the shingle, but found nothing.

"I'm going to move around to the other side Jemma. You stay where you are, as it's a bit deeper out there and you're shorter than me."

"Be careful Frankie and don't stay long, as Dad may wake up and wonder where we are."

"Okay."

Dragging one foot in front of the other, Frankie made his way to the opposite side of the stones, his Wellington boots making it hard going, as they filled with water.

Suddenly he lost his footing and disappeared beneath the water. Surfacing again, he tried valiantly to grab at the shingle bank but the stones kept rolling into the creek and he couldn't get a grip on them. Screaming out to Jemma to get Dad, he floundered around, trying to keep his head above water, while his boots weighed him down.

Jemma was yelling at the top of her lungs for Dad, who burst through the trees like a Rhinoceros searching for its young.

Stripping down to the waist, he quickly jumped into the freezing river and dragged Frankie out by the back of his shorts. Frankie spluttered and choked, coughing up the river water he had swallowed. To help him, Dad slapped him several times on the back, none too gently either and told Jemma to run back to their picnic spot, for dry towels.

Stripping Frankie of his wet clothes, he wrapped him in the towels, all the time telling him how stupid he had been, to try wading in the river in those huge boots. Frankie shivered and shook and looked very crestfallen.

"We were trying to search for gold that might have been missed by the diggers," he explained.

Dad wasn't having any of it.

"I told you that it all happened many years ago and didn't you think many people have probably searched this area, before we came."

"Sorry Dad, I thought it didn't look deep so I'd be alright. I forgot those boots would be so heavy, when they filled with water."

"Well the only thing to do now is head for home. I'm going to be in deep water with your Mum, for nearly letting you drown."

Quickly they packed up their gear and took to the trail once more. Poor Frankie felt dreadful, as he had spoilt their day out and though he was wrapped in the towels, he was still trying to get warm.

Reaching the road, Dad suggested they stop on the way back and get some fish and chips for tea.

"It will warm you up Frankie and at least the fishing exhibition won't return home without any fish!!"

The sad and sorry pair cheered up at the thought.

Swimming Race

By Brianna Dobson age 11

"Take your marks."

BEEP! Off we go diving into the pool. Suddenly as I hit the water everything rushes out of my mind. The water is warm but I shiver with adrenaline.

"What am I doing?" I think to myself. "Freestyle or breaststroke? That's right, breaststroke."

By now it is too late to do my pull out that helps me move quickly like a shark moving though the water after its prey. Up down, up down the rhythm keeps on going over and over in my head. I am nearly finished.

Since I was a little girl I have always wanted to swim competitively. I have been training so hard to get the best results that I can. Now I am at Manawatu Age Group Championships and Mum and I have travelled over to Palmerston North for this event.

I had been at Age Groups last year but this year I am a whole lot faster and fitter. Earlier I had been hanging out with my friends when the man on the speaker said, "Event 14. Swimmers can you please come up to the marshaling tent."

I looked down at my hand which had all my event numbers on it. Event 14 was written in thick black pen. I had to go up to the marshaling tent. When I got over there they started calling out the names and what lane they were in. After a while they called out " Brianna Dobson". I went up and sat down. It was time to go up to the blocks now.

'Come on Brianna, you can do this.' I think to myself as I push myself nearer to the wall. I touch the wall. I have finished. After that is over and done with I feel so much more relaxed until I go back to Mum and the rest of the group. Nicole, my coach, asks me if I did the wrong pullout.

"No," I say, but I start to feel sick all over again. What if I got disqualified? I try my hardest not to think about it but my mind won't stop playing it over and over. I keep on trying to think happy thoughts but the words "disqualified" keep on repeating in my head like a nightmare that just won't go away. I am waiting for what seems like a lifetime for the results to come up. I keep on running back and forth from the tent to the results, then back to the tent and again to the results.

Finally the results come up. I gulp nervously. Everything seems to go into slow motion. I find my name, I have come third. I feel a rush of relief run down my spine. I run back to Mum, Nicole and the group.

"Mum," I cry, "I came third".

"Well done," Mum says.

Standing on the podium, I feel so proud of myself. Everyone was smiling up at me. When I leave the podium, Mum, Nicole and the rest of the group congratulate me. I feel like a movie star walking down the red carpet.

"Thank goodness that is over," I quietly say to myself. I am fine for the rest of the day.

The magnificent adventure of a delusional cat

By Phoebe Freya Harris age 17.

Based on the true story of our cat, Boy.

Dedicated to all those affected and still suffering from theChristchurch Earthquake and the many aftershocks that followed.

"Take hope that amazing things happen and don't give¨ up."

Bev Harris

A blur of black and white speeds up to Summit Road, distancing itself from the tremors of the scary earthquake. Driven by fear, fury and fright he works himself further away from the lights. Wandering around to find some kind of peace, he settles in a field with towering trees.

Away from his owners, away from the warmth he searches endlessly for the place he was found. A place without destruction, grief and confusion, a place located within the very same region. This cat has a big adventure to be told, it includes the struggles, the kindness and the tragedy he found. His name is Boy and with a lot of courage and strength, he struggled through the worst year any creature could have.

Chapter One

A holidaying family was greeted by a lost, wandering kitten. Found in a car park, alone and abandoned. The girl bent down and gave him a pat. They went to leave, but he wasn't having that. He followed them home, all 3.4 kilometers. They decided that love is found in peculiar places. This cat was no ordinary cat. He lived without daily food, a clean bed and a warm home. He often wondered why he'd been left, why he'd been forgotten while no other cat had.

Once he had decided that he could stay, the papers, and vets checked to see if he'd run away. No one had tried to find this special cat with the black spot around his eye. He was taken to a city, very different from where he was found, with these tall staggering buildings, the traffic, the crowds. He was greeted by a cat with a silky grey coat, who hissed at his presence, who growled at his purr.

He was excited to explore his very new home. Every day brought a great adventure for this young, joyful cat. A passing butterfly turned into a game. He chased it around the garden, leaping in the air. He followed the black and white dog around the back garden. He played in wardrobes and sat on the kitchen table. He walked into rooms, letting a deep, loud purr out, as he sat near the fire, curled up on the couch.

Chapter Two

One day, his happiness vanished as with the smashing of glass wear and picture frames came sadness. Books were thrown to the floor, bookcases joined them shortly after. Anything valuable was smashed into tiny fragments, scattered all across the floor. Items of nostalgia were thrown everywhere. The chimney seemed to get ripped from the roof, tiles fell, and windows shook. Seconds of an earthquake ruined everything throughout the house, the sound so deafening and frightening, you'd do anything to get out. The first instinct was to run for cover, away from the windows, ceilings that could fall. He ran towards the cat flap. He quickly escaped, but outside was no safer than the inside of a grizzly bears cave. The cliffs started to fall apart; the rocks tumbled and fell from their places. The sound was like an eruption, a sound much louder than we can imagine. The panic, confusion and stress were too much to handle, he couldn't find his owners, or the other animals. He raced up the hill to the Summit Road. And so this is where Boy's adventure started, with a horrible fright.

Chapter Three

The destruction was vast and everywhere. It affected wildlife, nature and created human despair. Boy raced far away from the noise of destruction, he saw the huge cliffs and the debris below them. He thought to himself that he must race to the top, where nothing could fall on him, and nothing could hurl from the sky. He looked behind him, expecting danger. He blinked away the dust left by the huge boulders. His black and white coat was getting coated by dirt. There was no time to stop to clean himself anymore. He must hurry.

He reached the top, but did not stop there. He surveyed the area, unsure where to go. His adrenaline moved him forward.

Chapter Four

He survived on passing mice, birds and frogs. He slept under bushes, he hid up in trees. All the while his owners searched endlessly. Posters were plastered on each of the empty street corners, shelters were searched. They held on to the hope that he'd find his way back.

Boy found the days merged into one, searching for food and water became his only goal. Through snowstorms, hail, rain, and sun, Boy watched the seasons begin to repeat. The leaves began to fall, and the icy frosts reappeared once again. His beautiful black and white spotty coat begun to thicken in preparation, for the harsh winter winds, and the cold winter nights. He meowed to the moon, he let out a cry. He was tired of running away from the threat of danger, he was tired of the aftershocks which reminded him his only aim was to survive.

Boy had lived his life on the top of the Summit Road; a year and a half had passed. He was aware of the increasing cold; he would suddenly run, accepting anyone's kindness that was offered to him. He dreamed of home, love and comfort, and what he would do for the family he once took for granted.

Chapter Five

After over a year and a half of worrying had finally passed, when a phone call from a stranger gave hope at last. Boy was safe, he was fed and he was finally out of danger. They approached the building, they looked in the cage. A great burst of happiness took place of the sadness that weighed. He was nervous and anxious, his spirit had gone. He was taken home, fed and the love was still strong. The grey cat and black and white dog watched him with curiosity, intrigued by the time he had been away from their family. He felt he didn't belong anymore, the danger still surging in the quiet, still home. He was locked inside, he stared out the window.

Weeks past and he grew a healthy size, he was finally released and took off by twilight. He raced up the hill, he reached the Summit Road. He felt safe and secure reminded by his home place. How he missed the quiet town, its land stretched for miles. He pretended he was there now, which helped him feel calm. A day passed, he felt more alone, then he heard an engine, and a calling sound. He came out slowly at first, afraid of the noise, but recognised one of his owners and ran towards her as fast as he could. He jumped in the car, and off they went home. Him purring and pleased that he wasn't alone. He was tired of fending only for himself; he wanted to be with his family again.

The adventure he had, we can only imagine, the emptiness he had felt, and a great sense of danger.

Chapter Six

Driven down the hill, back to the house, became a routine for this unhappy cat. He hated being restricted from the hill that waited. He would go outside then go up the hill again. Waiting by a fence for his owners to com, sitting on the passenger's knee as he stared at the fast moving scenery outside the window.

They did this each week despite the cost of petrol. All through his struggles, his changed personality, the cost of his care, Boy had a family, a family that cared.

Boy wasn't the only animal who struggled to cope; many of the animals around him had seemed to have lost hope. A decision was made, after three years of exisiting, the family would move to the little cottage in Waimate.

Chapter Seven

Goodbye's were said, loose ends were tied. They accepted that their leaving was the best way to find peace in the chaos that was their everyday lives. History was created in the Christchurch earthquake; destruction, grief and loss were left in its wake.

Every animal and person suffered in different ways, whether it was emotionally or physically, but they kept going each day. Boy was lucky in the way he found hope in a quiet corner in the south of our beautiful Aotearoa.

He spends his days purring as loud as a passing van, playing in the shadows and finding fun each day. His paw splashes in the pond, watching the fish. His head bobs as he follows their movements near the lily pads, hiding in the deep.

His personality continues to grow each day; only a sudden movement reminds him of the earthquake and the aftermath that remains. His adventure is not completely written in stone. There are things that you and I will never know. Boy learnt that the friendship and love he shared with his family, the dog and the angry grey cat are the most important things that he could have in the end.

We can do this!

By Jutta Heitland (translated from the German by Sue McRae)

Once upon a time there was a primary school boy named Toby, who was nearly the tallest in his class. One day, right in the middle of class, there was a knock at the door. Mr Berger, the school principal, walked in with a new child saying: "This is David – a new boy for your class."

The whole class giggled and David went bright red.

"Come over here, David and have a seat in the front row", said Ms Gorman, the class teacher. The class couldn't help giggling again. David was rather short and he had the kind of unruly hair that sticks out in all directions.

Mr Berger left them to it, and lessons continued until morning break. The children raced outside, leaving David all by himself. So he went outside on his own and stood quietly in a corner of the playground.

You should still be in kindergarten, you little tot!" yelled one boy. Everyone laughed. David went bright red and said nothing.

"Haven't you learnt how to talk yet?" jeered the boy.

"Course I have", said David. But then the bell went and the children returned to class.

At home later that day, Toby talked about the new kid in his class and mentioned how everyone had laughed at him. His mother took it very seriously.

"Look after David a bit, will you, Toby. It can't be easy for him, you know" she said.

"Nah, why should it have to be me?" asked Toby.

"Because you're bigger than him and you can help David. Go on, just make an effort."

"But I don't want to!" yelled Toby defiantly.

Next day at school he sat in his usual place beside Philip. Then David walked into the classroom and a few of the children started laughing again: "Look, here comes the dwarf."

David instantly went bright red again. Then a few children taunted him with: "What's up beetroot boy?"

Toby suddenly became very agitated; he could feel his heart pounding. He and Philip looked at each other. Toby eventually picked up a book and opened it while Philip calmly sat there watching the other children.

"What's going on here then?" came the stern voice of Ms Gorman. The whole class immediately fell silent.

That day David went home and said to his mother, "That school's really dumb. I'm never going back there."

"Why ever not?" asked his mother.

"The children all laugh at me because I'm so little."

"Oh dear, but you have to go to school, whether you want to or not. Do all the children really laugh at you?"

"Apart from Philip they all do. Toby just goes along with them a bit, but the others are totally mean to me."

David gulped and began to cry. His mother put her arm around him and tried to cheer him up.

"Okay," she said finally, "I'm going to phone Philip now. Maybe he will have time to play with you today."

David's mother phoned Philip's mother, who immediately invited David to come over and play. When Philip heard her, he was really angry and started complaining.

"David shouldn't come here. He's dumb. I don't want to play with him. Anyway, Toby will be here too today. What do you think he'll have to say about it?"

"Oh come on now, that's enough of that. Don't make such a fuss," said his mother.Then the doorbell went. It was David.

"Oh well, I suppose you'd better come in then," said Philip gruffly.

David walked in very timidly and was still standing in the hallway when the doorbell went again.

"Oh, that's bound to be Toby," said Philip cheerfully and opened the door.

When Toby saw David he laughed.

"Oh boy, what on earth is red-face doing here?"

David's eyes immediately filled with tears. He turned and ran as fast as he could down the stairs and out onto the street.

"Quick, chase him!" yelled Philip and he and Toby ran after David.

They saw David running full speed down the street and Toby suddenly called out, "Stop, wait! Don't run any further, David!" but it was too late. David fell into a deep hole that had suddenly opened up in front of him, and disappeared.

Toby and Philip ran to the edge of it and looked down inside the gaping hole. They couldn't see anything. It was all pitch black.

"What do we do now?" asked Philip.

"Don't ask me," said Toby, his voice trembling. He was feeling guilty for making fun of David earlier.

"Come on then, let's go down the hole," he suggested finally.

"And how do we do that?" asked Philip.

"This way of course," said Toby, pulling a blue climbing rope out of his pocket. Together they clambered down the steep hole towards the bottom.

Once they got to the bottom, they saw that it was no longer dark inside, but glistening and shimmering in every colour you could possibly imagine. In front of them stood David. He hadn't hurt himself when he fell; he was just standing there staring very hard at something in the corner.

Philip and Toby moved closer out of curiosity and saw lots of tiny dwarves approaching them with the same degree of interest.

"We are the dwarves from the undercity. Who are you?" asked the dwarves in high-pitched voices. Before the three boys could answer, they heard a deeper, more serious voice demanding to know,

"What are you doing here in my undercity world?"

Terrified, and with their hearts racing, the three boys turned around to find themselves staring straight into the good-natured eyes of an old wizard. He was quite serious, but he winked his right eye at them in a friendly way.

"So tell me, do. How did you come to be in my world?"

"I think I must be dreaming," said Toby.

"No, you're not dreaming," answered the wizard. "How did you manage to worm your way in here?"

"Ah, well, we didn't mean to at all," stuttered Philip, "We just fell down the hole."

"Well, well! Tell the truth now, you got here on Toby's blue climbing rope, didn't you?" asked the wizard.

"Um, yes, but only because we wanted to rescue David!" exclaimed Toby.

David stood there, bright red in the face, as always.

"Now let me see, I have something here in my cape for David. You will no doubt have a good use for it."

The wizard reached into the fold of his shimmering blue cape and pulled out a golden violin.

"Wow, that's awesome!" cried Philip and Toby in unison.

"Here David, this is for you. You already know what to do with it."

The wizard gave David the violin and said, "There you are, and now please leave, all of you."

"But how will we find our way out?" asked the children.

"David can show you the way," answered the wizard. "And Speedy will help you too. Speedy! Come here a minute, will you!"

"I'm already here!" piped up a little voice that belonged to a tiny dwarf no bigger than a mouse.

"Speedy, please accompany these three boys on their way out and don't forget the test."

"Leave it to me. Come along, boys!" cried Speedy and shot away.

They walked along a dark, wet passageway. It was a bit creepy, but the boys didn't want to let their feelings show. Then to their horror, without any warning, they saw a big, black gate in front of them, guarded by three terrifying dragons, all grunting loudly and breathing fire.

"Oh hell! Now we're in trouble," whispered Toby.

"Only David can help us now," answered Speedy. "Otherwise, we don't have a chance."

The dragons kept breathing fire, trying to strike the foursome with their flames. It was extremely difficult to dodge them. Philip couldn't stand it any longer. He yelled, "Come on, David, do something for goodness sake!"

"Oh, but what could our little friend here possibly do? He should still be in kindergarten," said Toby disparagingly.

David went bright red again, then picked up the golden violin and began to play. It was a song the boys had never heard before, with a wonderful, lilting melody. As if by magic, the dragons lay down and fell asleep.

"I can't believe my eyes," said Toby. "How come you know how to play the violin anyway?"

"I just can," replied David.

Then the big black gate opened and the four were able to walk through it. A very dark, musty passageway awaited them, at the end of which they could see a shining light. The three boys and Speedy approached it and suddenly noticed everything was as light as day. Weren't they still underground?

"How could that have happened?" asked Toby.

"Above or below ground, it's all the same in the end," laughed Speedy.

They walked past a green meadow brimming with flowers of every colour until they came to a fast-running stream.

"So this is where it all ends," said Philip. "We'll never be able to get to the other side."

"Yes we will," said David, "If we just use Toby's rope. We can throw it across to the other side of the stream and then clamber our way across."

"Good idea," said Toby and immediately tried to throw one end of the rope to the other side of the stream. But no matter how many times he tried, he couldn't do it.

"Now what?" he asked.

"There's only one thing for it," said Speedy. "Tie the rope around your middle, we'll stay here and hold onto you tight, while you can swim across to the other side."

"Okay", nodded Toby uneasily, "but I don't feel good about this."

He tied the rope around himself and plunged into the fast-flowing stream. The water lapped over his head and he struggled to catch his breath, but eventually swam through the raging torrent to reach the other side.

One by one the others followed, with David valiantly clutching his violin above the churning water.

Eventually they all made it over to Toby on the other side. They were shivering with cold, because the water was freezing. But as they walked on, trembling, a warm wind suddenly came up and soon dried them off again.

As pleasant as the wind was to start with, it soon picked up speed and turned into a real storm, more violent than any wind the three boys and Speedy had ever experienced.

"Help me, you lot!" cried Speedy suddenly, before being catapulted through the air. Philip quickly reached out for him and just managed to grab Speedy by the tip of his pointy little cap. Speedy scuttled into the pocket of Philip's jacket trembling with fear.

They walked on bent over double, struggling to stand up in the wind, until Toby cried: "Oh no, it just gets worse and worse!"

He pointed to a swarm of huge, black, screeching birds threatening to dive-bomb onto the heads of the four. They screamed in fear of their lives, ducked and ran on as fast as they could. Toby yelled: "Please play the violin, David! Maybe you can calm them down!"

David couldn't stand up holding the violin because the wind was too strong. So he knelt down and played. Amazingly, the birds turned around and flew off screeching in the other direction.

"Look over there!" cried Philip.

He pointed to a nearby plant with huge leaves. When they reached the plant, they crawled under the first leaf that was big enough to cover them completely, as protection from the wind. They waited a while. All four of them were very anxious. They all thought the same thing: what does this all mean?

"What does all this mean?" David finally put it into words.

"Speedy, you must have some idea."

"Unfortunately not much," answered Speedy, "only that it is probably one of many tests."

"Not more tests," wept Philip suddenly. "I want to go home!"

"Don't cry, Philip, we can do this!" said Toby in an attempt to reassure him. He looked around. The storm had let up a bit.

"Look over there!" he cried, pointing in front of them to a cave that was very close by. "Let's go and hide in there."

Toby stood up and the other three exhausted boys followed him into the cave. It smelt musty in the cave and it was bitterly cold.

"This is horrible," complained David now too.

"Wait up," said Speedy and dug a deep hole in the wet earth of the cave floor. The three boys were curious to see what he was doing and drew closer. When the hole was finished, Speedy reached into his trouser pocket and pulled out a very small blue cloth. He unfolded it — over and over again. The little piece of cloth became bigger and bigger until it was large enough to be a perfect fit for the hole.

"Wow!" whispered the three stricken boys.

"Now close your eyes," ordered Speedy. All three of them closed their eyes and waited.

"You may open them now," they heard Speedy say.

The boys could not believe their eyes. The finest food and drink was now laid out on the big blue cloth. Next to it there were four sleeping bags, and in the corner they could see a funny little campfire burning that made the cave feel like a cosy, warm refuge.

"Wow!" managed Toby, stunned by it all.

"That's amazing!" cried Philip and David.

"How in the world did you do it?" The three boys asked inquisitively.

"That's my secret," answered Speedy, "But eat up now before it gets cold."

They didn't need to be told twice and hungrily devoured everything down to the very last crumb. Then they snuggled into their sleeping bags. Before they fell asleep, Philip whispered to David: "Hey David, I think you're cool, do you want to be friends?"

David gulped. He was quite taken aback. Nobody had ever asked him something like that before.

"Yeah, you bet," he said. Then Toby gave him a friendly smile and said, "David, I'd like to be your friend too."

David's eyes pricked with tears of joy.

"Thanks," he whispered. And with a warm feeling inside and out, the three friends fell asleep by the gentle light of the fire. Speedy had been quietly listening to them and shut his eyes with a smile too.

Next morning when they woke up, a delicious breakfast was already waiting for them on the magic blue cloth. They felt like they were starving again and eagerly tucked in. Then Speedy folded up the cloth again as carefully as he had unfolded it the day before, until it was small enough to fit back into his trouser pocket.

"Where shall we head to now?" he asked happily, because the three boys had been staring at him completely awestruck by the way he was folding the cloth.

"Your blue cloth is amazing. I wish I had one like that too," said Toby wistfully.

"I can quite believe that. But which way do we go from here?" repeated Speedy.

"Not in the direction of that storm, that's for sure," said Toby determinedly. "Let's look for a different way out."

The other boys nodded in agreement and set off in the direction of a faint light they could set at the other end of the cave. It was the way out on the other side. But it turned out to be a narrow little hole, as they discovered when they got there. They squeezed their way out through the tight gap and saw three different paths in front of them, one going left, one going straight ahead and one going right.

"And what do we do now?" asked David.

"I vote we take the middle one," said Toby after some thought, "What do you think?"

"Actually I'm more in favour of the one on the right," said David. Speedy and Philip whispered to each other. Finally they both said, "We reckon the left."

"Okay," decided Toby. "Let's split up. I'm going to take the middle path, anyway."

"Wait a sec there," interrupted Speedy. "Let's take some time to think about this first."

So they all sat down and had a think.

"I've got it!" cried David finally. "I don't think it's a good idea for us to split up. We're pretty strong as a foursome and it could get very dangerous for us on our own. How about we all go down each path together? Then we'll soon find out which is the right one."

"That sounds sensible," said Philip.

Toby and Speedy nodded in agreement.

They began by going right. That path was lined with two high walls on either side and they couldn't see over them. After about five hundred metres they came up against another wall right in front of them.

"Ok then, we'll just have to turn around," said Speedy.

So they turned around and tried out the middle path. Exactly the same thing happened. About five hundred metres down the path, they came up against another wall they could not get past.

"Ok then, we'll just have to turn around," said Philip this time.

The left-hand path they took last started out just like the other two. But after a while, it began to branch out.

"And now – what do we do now?" asked Speedy. Philip and David had no idea. Toby thought very hard.

"I know!" he suddenly yelled with excitement. "We're inside a maze! And there's only one thing to do: keep to the right and follow the wall all the way. That's the only way we'll ever get out of here again."

"How do you know that?" asked Philip. "Maybe we are just hopelessly lost?"

"You've got to believe me, please! I just know. My father told me that and it always works, honestly!" cried Toby.

"I think we're just going to have to do what Toby says. We don't have any other choice," said David.

"I think so too," agreed Speedy.

"Oh well, let's give it a try," relented Philip.

So together they kept going and held right the whole way. After two hours in the blinding heat, Philip groaned.

"I can't go any further. Your suggestion was never right in the first place, Toby!"

"Yes it was," replied Toby.

Since they had no other choice, they kept on going. Finally the end was in sight. Greatly relieved, they rushed towards the exit; then they saw a vast area of sand in front of them.

"I can't take any more!" cried Philip in desperation. "I think I'm going mad here! Man, this here is a desert!"

"Stop yelling so much, we can see that for ourselves," replied Toby grumpily.

"But I'm thirsty. I want something to drink," whined Philip.

"Stop whining!" cried Toby.

"We're all thirsty," said David. "Please let's just be quiet and think for a minute instead of arguing."

"Look over there!" yelled Speedy. "Do you see that red mountain? There's bound to be some shade there, let's go and have a rest."

With their last ounce of energy, they dragged themselves over to the mountain and sat down in the shade, exhausted.

"Do you think we'll ever make it home again?" asked David.

"Course we will," said Toby quickly, but he had an uneasy feeling about it too.

Philip meanwhile had climbed up to the top of the red mountain and was about to wave to his friends when the mountain suddenly started moving.

"Oh God, what was that!" he yelled before hurtling back down again. He landed right by his friends and they all stood up now and watched wide-eyed at what was happening. A head that had obviously been buried below the surface suddenly poked up out of the sand and a turtle with four huge feet and a thunderous voice loomed over them, demanding to know: "Who is it who dares disturb my peace and quiet?"

"David, quick, play your violin!" cried Toby.

"Don't be silly! Nothing and no one can help us now! We have to run away!" cried David in fear of his life.

"Please David! You're the only one who can help us now!" Toby tried to persuade him.

"Toby's right. You can tame wild animals," pleaded Speedy.

The thunderous voice of the turtle again demanded, "Who's that disturbing my peace and quiet, is what I want to know!"

David quickly raised his violin and began to play. The turtle immediately stared swaying in time to the music. It hummed away quietly to itself and finally said in a much more friendly tone of voice,

"My name's Aurora, what can I do for you?"

"We want to go home!" cried Philip in desperation.

"Oh, and where's that?" asked Aurora in a deep, lilting voice.

"We don't know either, but we think it must be somewhere beyond this desert."

Toby gazed quietly into the dusky eyes of the turtle.

Somewhere – wait a minute," said Aurora, looking at Speedy with raised eyebrows. "Don't I know you from somewhere?"

"Yes, we've met before. I'm Speedy, and if there's anyone at all who can help us now, it's you!"

"I haven't moved from here for 10,000 years. Do you even know what you're asking me to do! But oh well. Since it's you, Speedy, I will see what I can do. Come on then, climb aboard, you lot!" thundered Aurora.

They quickly clambered onto Aurora's back and she started slowly moving forward in long, loping strides.

"Can't she go any faster? It's going to take ages at this rate," complained Toby softly.

"For goodness sake, boy!" growled Aurora, "Don't you know that one of my steps is worth a thousand of yours? Now be quiet or I'll make you all do it on foot from here on in!"

Toby went bright red with shame and softly muttered, "Sorry."

The three boys and Speedy tried to make themselves as comfortable as possible. But it was hot, and the sun shone down relentlessly. They sweated in the heat and became very thirsty. Just when they thought they couldn't last any longer, night began to settle in. And as much as they had sweated all day, they now began to freeze.

They heard Aurora's deep voice booming: "Is anyone here cold?"

"Yes, we're all freezing up here," shivered David.

"OK, then get under the shell, all of you!" ordered Aurora.

"No, I'm not going under there. That's too weird for me," whined Philip.

"Oh, let's at least give it a go!" suggested Toby and Speedy said, "Yes, Toby's right."

So they all crawled under the shell of the turtle and were surprised how warm and snug it was under there. It felt nice and cosy beneath the shell, and the wrinkly skin of the turtle rubbed against their skin, thawing them out. Eventually they fell asleep, exhausted.

They didn't wake up again until they heard Aurora's thunderous voice. "So here we are then. There's the glass building at the end of the desert."

Through tired eyes, the friends peered out to see a huge building ahead of them made entirely of glass.

Aurora stopped and called out, "Everyone out now, and make it snappy!"

The boys and Speedy hurried to get out from under the turtl, who immediately turned around and headed off back to where she had come from.

"Thank you, and see you again soon!" the children called out to Aurora. She turned her head.

"I should hope not," she said, winking her dusky eyes at them. "But here's one more piece of advice for you, do what Lederhose says now!"

Toby didn't give up, calling out, "But won't we see you again?"

"Oh, no," said Aurora quietly, "That's not possible. Only in our dreams will we be able to see one another again."

"Oh, that's a pity. Well, bye then, and take care," said Toby quietly.

"Bye Toby, you're all on the right track no," replied Aurora and set off on the return leg.

Deep in thought, the three friends walked with Speedy towards the glass building. What did Aurora mean about Lederhose? They entered the building and were amazed to find the biggest glass maze they had ever seen.

"That's so beautiful," said Philip, visibly moved.

"Yes, and I know how we're going to get through it!" cried David, confidently.

"Always keep to the right," laughed the other three and ran off to try it out.

Less than ten minutes later, they had already reached the exit. And who should be there with a look of amazement on his face? Lederhose! Lederhose was a boy who always wore traditional leather shorts with a built-in leather bib, day and night, winter or summer. Lederhose started laughing and called out, "Hey Speedy, it's been ages since we last met."

"That's true," said Speedy, and the two hugged each other in delight.

"Who's that you have there with you?" asked Lederhose out of curiosity. "They seem to be world champion maze busters!"

"The three of them will have to fill you in themselves," said Speedy in a rough, low voice, "For sadly I now have to say goodbye. My work here is done."

"But why, Speedy?" asked the three astonished friends. "Why can't you just come with us?"

"Because I have to go back now," replied Speedy sadly. "You three know that you can rely on one another and you're good friends now. That's all that counts. So goodbye now, but please don't forget about me altogether."

He gave each of the three boys a parting handshake. Toby gulped, David quietly shed a tear and Philip asked, "When will we see you again?"

"Only in your dreams," said Speedy sadly.

"Take care, Speedy," said Toby. "We'll miss you."

"Go now with Lederhose, he'll show you the way. It's not far now," Speedy bowed slightly and then went back through the glass building.

The three boys were sad to see him go.

"Come along now," said Lederhose cheerfully, snapping them out of that mood. "You see, I still have one more surprise in store for you." The three doleful comrades set off rather reluctantly after Lederhose. He led them to a hole in the ground.

"You have to go down there now," grinned Lederhose.

"Why can't you stop grinning?" asked Toby.

"Well, because I can't wait to see whether you dare to do it," laughed Lederhose.

"Dare to do what?" asked Philip.

"Jump down the hole!" cried Lederhose and laughed yet again.

The three boys looked down and could see only a gaping, black hole that seemed to have no end. They looked at each other.

"Is there no other way?" asked Toby quietly.

"Speedy told you to trust me, didn't he?" smiled Lederhose. "It's the only chance you have to get back home again. All you have to do is have faith in yourselves, so jump in and see where it takes you."

"Ok, let's do it then," said David. "We don't have any other choice."

"Ok then," agreed Toby. "If we stick together, we can do this."

All three boys lined up next to one another in front of the black hole. Without any discussion, they all held hands.

"See you, Lederhose!" they said.

"Best of luck!" cried Lederhose. "See you soon!"

The three boys jumped, but what happened next was something they would never have thought possible. No sooner had they jumped than they landed in a big, spiral chute that was longer than anything they had ever seen before. They yelled and whooped as they spun around, because it was so much fun. But at the end of the slide they could see a huge, gaping hole coming towards them, faster and faster, and they hurtled towards it at breakneck speed, screaming at the top of their lungs.

"Toby, time to get up!" called the voice of his little sister Sophie. "It's nearly time for school."

"Sophie, is that you?" asked Toby, in a daze, "Is that really you?"

"Course it is," laughed Sophie. "You're acting a bit weird today."

"My God,' thought Toby. 'Then everything that happened must have been a dream."

He got up, had breakfast and set off for school. When he reached the classroom, he met up with his two friends, who smiled at him a little uncertainly. And who would have thought? There in the classroom sat Lederhose, waving at them with a cheery smile on his face.

The bell rang for the start of class. Before they went to their seats, David whispered to Philip and Toby, "Did you two dream about Speedy too?"

Toby and Philip nodded, their hearts racing. It was simply impossible! How could it have happened?

During morning break, the three of them met up with Lederhose. The foursome then stood in a circle all stacking hands in the middle, one on top of the other.

"We're friends for life now!" they chorused.

And that's the way they stayed …

<u>You Have Nine Days To Go</u>

By Charlotte Jewell age 11.

"You have nine days to go."
The voice kept ringing in Kathy's ears.

"What does it mean?" asked Jessie with a look of fear in her eyes.

"How did this all happen?"

Kathy and Jessie had somehow been taken to a place. A place of darkness. Where was it? Well, neither of them knew. Kathy and Jessie were the only ones there. None of it made sense, they could not figure out why or how they had got there. They had been living normal lives and then suddenly there was a flash and they were taken to this bizarre world.

It had been nearly a day now and last night they both had a dream, more like a nightmare where an evil voice boomed "You have nine days to go." And then, they woke up.

"It must mean something," Jessie said as she cautiously looked underneath an evil-looking blackberry bush and saw the rotting body of a rat.

"AHH!" she screamed and jumped back in fright. "This place is so creepy!"

They wandered around for a while before Kathy spotted a trail of blackberries. They looked like they were glowing. It could have been their eyes playing tricks on them but they followed it, unthinkingly. They subconsciously walked like zombies, eyes glued to the trail. It finally led them to a door, the most massive door Jessie had ever seen, but Kathy kept going. Bang! She hit the gigantic structure.

"Oh! There's a door there." She said, stunned.

"Uh yeah." Jessie replied. "It's kinda hard to miss".

"Well let's open it then!" Kathy exclaimed.

They tried to pull on the humongous, heavy handle but something stopped them. Jessie noticed a small button on the bottom right hand corner of the door.

"No," she said. "Don't press it, I've had enough creepy things happen today, or tonight, we need a break."

They found a small, sheltered area to sleep and despite all of the weird happenings over the previous two days, they got to sleep quite easily.

"You have eight days to go."

The voice boomed. Again, they woke up together and simultaneously they said "Eight days until what?"

"Maybe it's something to do with that door" said Kathy.

She got up and reached for the button. For a second there was nothing, but then there was an ear-piercing creak and the door revealed some sort of puzzle. The room was gigantic with walls as tall as a skyscraper and the floor was covered with patterns. The puzzle was a big round concrete slab in the middle of the floor. It had giant handles that would slide around but not lift off the slab. Jessie's first thought was that they had to move them in a specific pattern, but how would they ever discover it?

Jessie tripped over one of the handles and as she fell onto a square shape on the slab, there was a short melody that went "da-de-da-de-dum."

"Well, that was strange" said Kathy just as she stepped onto a circle shape. There was another melody "de-de-de-do-dum-de-do."

"Hey, that sounded familiar," said Jessie and so she stepped onto a triangle – "do-do-do-do-dooooo."

"The dream!" she exclaimed.

"What? What dream?" replied Kathy, confused.

"The music, it's from the dream! It was playing in the background when the creepy voice was talking!" Jessie yelled. "Hey, maybe we need to play the whole song, by stepping on the different shapes!"

"Oh, well let's try some patterns then!" Kathy cried.
She tried a combination – triangle, circle, triangle, square.

"That's nearly it!" screamed Jessie excitedly "But what about triangle, circle, square, triangle?"

Incredulously, it worked! A portal appeared in the middle of the room, it was a red, rectangular window and the air inside was glowing, just like the blackberries. Jessie and Kathy looked at each other. They joined hands, held their breath and together stepped into the portal. They heard a whooshing sound and saw a blazing flash.

Inexplicably, they were back to their ordinary lives, sitting at the dinner table, a half-eaten bowl of spaghetti in front of them. It seemed that time had stood still.

That night just as they fell asleep they both had a dream. "You have seven days to go"....

KIDSTUFF

By Jean McDavitt. (1st Adult)

"James, James, your father's ready to go. Are you going with him?"

"Blast," muttered James under his breath. Didn't they know he was much too busy to go to the match with Dad. Perhaps if he kept quiet, said nothing, they might forget about him.

"James! Hurry up boy. He won't wait much longer."

James put his head down, pretending that they were not there, waiting impatiently by the front door. His unfinished homework was spread over the unmade bed. The curtains were tightly drawn against the sunlight which also persisted in trying to interrupt him. The walls of his bedroom were hung with cut-outs from computer magazines. Sneakers, socks and clothes were strewn about the floor. As usual his door was tightly shut with the DO NOT DISTURB sign securely in place.

"J-a-a-mes!"

"I wish they would just go, leave me alone," he murmured. "I wish I never had to leave you."

He put out his hand to stroke his beloved computer and jumped as the door crashed open behind him. His fingers touched a never before combination of keys and for a moment all went dark.

"James. We are not leaving you home again. This time you're coming with us. James! Where are you?"

He turned to speak to his mother and to his surprise realised that a bright blue screen was between them. He watched with interest as she ran around the room, checking inside the wardrobe, under the bed and behind the curtains. She called to someone in the passage behind her, and left the room again.

"He's not here. I wonder where he is? Not like him to go away from his computer, and look, John, he hasn't even started his homework. I don't know what's going to become of that boy. He worries me."

Dad stuck his nose into the room for a moment then disappeared. James could hear his voice as they moved away.

"I'm not waiting any longer. This is the last time I'll ever ask him to come to a match with me, Buying that damn computer is the worst thing we've ever done. Never had two sensible words out of him since the day it came into the house."

"He might be in the bathroom."

"No! I'm off. He's your son – you look after him."

"Good. They've gone."

James took a step and hit his knee on the screen. He walked right around the outside edge, sure that somewhere there must be a gap he could slip through, back into his bedroom, but it was sealed tight. He looked around him and realised that he was surrounded by winking lights, thousands of pieces of brightly coloured wire and pieces of plastic, all with different numbers written on them. A humming sound filled his ears. With a shock he realised that he was *inside* his computer.

How could he get out?

Travel! That was it. He knew from the hours he had spent searching the web that there was plenty of 'Travel' in here. All he needed to do was connect with it and he could be out. He carefully touched one of the coloured lights.

"I wonder what will happen if I just say the word?" he wondered. "Why isn't there a keyboard in here, so I can just type the question?"

'Travel,' he said aloud. What a reaction! He was picked up and spun around. All the places in the world revolved around him. It was scary.

"I don't like this space," he cried and instantly was spun out into space. Stars, comets, solar systems rushed by him, along with tons of space junk. A satellite station was off to his left and as it passed he could see the astronauts through the cut away section.

"Stop!" he called, and slowly he stopped moving.

"Wow, I didn't think much of that," he thought. "How can I get out of here. Maybe I can email myself somewhere. Perhaps this green button . . ."

Gently he placed his finger on the button. "Better not be too loud. I don't want to go through that again." He whispered an email address, someone he often spent time chatting to. But he must have made a mistake.

He spun for a brief moment then gasped in surprise as, through the screen, he looked into the eyes of a jet black African man. James waved his arm.

"Oh, Oh," said the stranger. "Don't like the look of this. Looks like some kind of computer virus. Better delete it straight-away." He disappeared.

"I'll try again," said James. He grinned when the spinning stopped and he saw his friend. What a Nerd. Sitting there all scrunched up in front of him, glasses fogged in concentration, finger nails bitten to the quick.

"Gosh, if I'd known she looked like that I wouldn't have wasted my time. Never mind, let's hope she can get me out of here."

He waved and watched fascinated as she frowned, stuck her tongue out, then bit her lip.

"Something is wrong," she muttered. "Don't like the look of this. All these J J J's. Must be an attachment. Be careful opening attachments," she muttered to herself. "No! I'm not going to risk it. Had enough trouble last time."

She pushed her Delete button and James was on his own again. He was beginning to feel peckish and he knew what he wanted. "Food," he shouted out loud.

A vast array of food appeared before him. Hamburgers, snails, peaches, fish and chips, roast chickens, cabbage, ice cream, rice dishes, pasta dishes, frogs legs, things he had never dreamed of but when he moved to pick up a peach he realised that all the brightly coloured food was only images.

"I'm hungry!" he moaned. "I want some real food not this make believe stuff." But nothing happened. Slowly the images faded away.

James was frightened now. Suppose he had to stay here forever and what was the life span of a computer, anyway. Dad said they depreciated at 30% so that meant that in only three years he might be past his use by date. He began to run around the area, knocking over things as he went. An unexpected noise made him look up. Thousands, no, millions of teeth were coming towards him. He cringed in terror. A voice spoke.

"What do you think you're doing, disturbing us at our work? How dare you get in our way."

"I'm sorry. Who are you?"

"Stupid boy. Think you know so much, spending all your time in the bedroom on your own, but, you don't know anything. Life is for living not looking at. Haven't you heard of bytes? That's what we are and we're going to get you."

James was terrified. His arms and legs shook and he feared that if he didn't get out of here soon he just might wet his pants and then what would happen? Everyone knew that you can't get a computer wet. It might blow up!

"He-e-e-l-p!" he screamed, at the top of his voice.

"What's the matter mate?"

A jolly little figure with big round eyes that rolled and eyelashes that fluttered was by his side. The bytes disappeared, but James knew they were only hiding. He had to get out of this place. He looked at the little man beside him and suddenly recognition struck him.

"I know you. You're the Help genie."

"That's right. What's your question?"

"How do I get out of here?"

The eyes rolled, first to the right, then to the left. Up and down they went and as James watched he thought the little fellow was going to turn himself inside out, so great were his contortions. Finally the movements stopped.

"I don't know! I can't find the answer in here. I've searched everywhere. No one has ever asked that before. Try again with another question."

"I don't have another question. I just want to go home, see my Mum and Dad again, have my dinner, go outside and play. In fact I wish I were at the football with Dad right now, instead of being lost in here."

Suddenly everything went dark. All the lights went out and the humming stopped. James heard a sigh. . .

"Computer's crashed."

He opened his eyes when the cheering started. Dad grabbed him and shook him delightedly.

"What do you think of that, eh? Winning goal. Gosh, it's good to see you smiling son. You had me a bit worried, sitting there all lost in your own little world, but I knew you would enjoy the game, if you came out with me."

James looked around him, listened to the noisy crowd, realised with vast relief that he was sitting safely beside Dad on the stand. He shut his eyes for a minute and relived once again the horror of being lost inside the computer, but he was safe now.

"Great game, Dad. Thanks for bringing me. I wonder what's for dinner, I'm starving, and Dad, after dinner can we have a game of cricket on the back lawn?"

Otakou Marae

By Prastutee Nepal age 9.

I stopped at the beautifully and delicately carved gate of *Otakou Marae*. The sun's golden sparkling warm rays shone brightly on my thoroughly brushed silky dark brown hair, making it look golden. A light breeze blew in my face as I opened my mouth slightly to breathe it in. The sea air tasted salty on my tongue. As we waited for the *karanga*, I suddenly felt very nervous. It was as if my tummy was a huge stony pit with spiders, snakes and mouldy skeletons with rabid rats running 'round. I shuddered. The thought was not a nice one.

I soon forgot about it, though, 'cause suddenly I heard a melodious voice split the air. It was the *Kai karanga* for the *tangata whenua!* Slow but steadily, I trudged up the path with my head facing the ground towards the beautifully carved marae. If I peeked from the corner of my eye I could see the emerald green ferns that daintily fringed and bordered the path. I could also just see the sapphire bluish-turquoise water of the harbor in the distance with a tiny layer of silvery mist above the sparkling water.

"Lovely!" I thought as I swivelled my head back up and continued hiking up the hill all the way to the front of the *marae*, shrugged off my bag and kicked off my shoes. I tiptoed quietly into the *wharenui* with its slanting wooden walls decorated with swiftly carved *tiki* and their rainbow and star struck *paua shell eyes* and cold wooden plank floor. I shivered. It was so cold. Outside, playing on the emerald green dew sprinkled grass with the warm sun on my back was where I wanted to be right now, not in the freezing cold *wharenui*!

"Still", I thought, "it can't be helped" and sunk down to the ground, next to my friend.

After a few speeches and *waiata,* it was my turn to do the *hongi*. Suddenly, I did not feel so good anymore. My knees wobbled like jelly, my teeth chattered nervously with fear. I was scared sick! I kept thinking of bad things like: Will our heads bang against each other? I did not want to do anything wrong! But then I remembered my teacher's advice.

"Go with the flow and here goes," I whispered, and marched up to the first person in the long line. Finally, it was all over. The *powhiri* was awesome!!!

Then it was time to do our *mihi.* I was really nervous. Finally, it was my turn. I shuffled slowly to the front and said my *mihi.* At the end of it, everyone smiled at me. I felt good. We also learned the *Maori* vowels, words, place name and how to pronounce them. We even learned how places got their names and that, in a Maori word, the word splits at the vowel. Then it was time for our next workshop which was: Learning how play *titi torea* and do the sequences. We started with a simple rhythm which got harder and harder each time. At the end we had a tournament to see who could do the sequence without dropping our *rakou* I dropped mine seconds after we started!

The last thing we did was making a Maori flute with Alex. We started by picking small little shoots of bamboo from the big bucket. I picked a smooth long slim piece of bamboo. After I finished pushing out the insides and drilled holes in it, I started to play the flute. Lovely music exploded out of it so it sounded as if a hundred songbirds were singing.

Then it was time to go. We played one last game, said a short prayer, thanked our hosts and rushed outside to get our bags and pull on our shoes. Then we bounded down the rocky path and out of the big lovely gate and boarded the bus. I glanced back at the *marae* as I stepped onto the steamy and dusty bus, knowing that I would always keep this memorable experience in my heart.

The Treehouse

By Laura Pedley age 12

Molly and Ben were twins and their family had just moved houses from Glenbell Street to Soup Street and they went out to explore their new backyard. In next to no time at all they spotted a giant tree in one of the neighbouring backyards and were busting to climb it so they set off in search of their parents to ask them if they would allow it.

But Mum said "NO WAY you are only 7 years old and you think that you can just wander off to somebody's backyard that we barely know. We would never allow that, and any way what were you two going to be doing there?"

"Well we spotted a giant tree and were wondering if we would be allowed to climb it," Molly replied.

"Climb a tree without supervision that is even worse! NO WAY!!"

"Oh please Mum," said Ben.

"NO! Now just go and play with the toys like good kids because can't you see that I am busy unpacking and look at how many boxes I've got!"

So, in much dismay, the twins went off in search of something else to do. They went off into the playroom to set up the remote control car racing track they had just got for Christmas from their grandparents. They loved it so much.

After about two hours the twins parents peeped through the hole in the door which was meant to house the door handle but it had not yet been installed. To the parents delight they saw their two adorable children playing with the cars in such a polite manner because they were kindly sharing the cars.

As the parents walked in, a shock shot to the children's face as they wondered why the parents were in there. Was it because they did something wrong or they had to go somewhere or was it because the parents had some boxes for them to unpack? It was none of them! To their surprise it was because the parents had noticed how quiet they had been and wanted to know if Molly and Ben would like to go to the neighbor's house and see the tree and possibly climb it!

Molly and Ben rapidly jumped to their feet and were bursting with excitement. They just couldn't wait to climb the tree. As the family entered the antique gate of the neighbouring house, they went to the front door. They entered with caution and to their surprise a boy from Ben's class answered the door! His name was Luke. With lots of enthusiasm Ben, Molly and Luke rush out to the backyard with no drama at all. They just wanted to climb that tree. The tree was quite big and very bushy. They thought it could be an Oak Tree.

When they had reached the third branch Molly and Ben's parents had appeared alongside Luke's Mum. "At last," Molly chanted as she reached the top of the giant. By the time all of the children had arrived at the top of the tree Molly had started to sing "I'm the King of the castle and you're the dirty rascal."

The others joined in. It began to turn dark so the children started to come down from the tree. They said their goodbyes and went back home to bed.

The next day Molly and Ben were up bright and early eating the warm porridge their mother made for them every morning! The clock struck ten o'clock and the children wandered round in search of something to do. They thought and thought until something appeared in their minds. They could go back next door to see Luke and maybe climb his tree again.

As they stood at the door of Luke's house an amazing idea popped into Ben's head. He spat it out with no time to lose. They could build a lookout or maybe even a tree house. Molly was not too sure about the idea but said, "Ask Luke first".

Luke again answered the door with no hesitation, and he yelled out to his Mum, "I am going out to play in the tree with Molly and Ben."

Mum replied, "Ok then but remember safety first".

While the children were walking out to the tree Ben hooked Luke in on their plan to build a tree house. Luke thought that that was an awesome idea but how were they going to do it by themselves? Ben suggested that they asked for some help from their fathers.

"My Dad would not mind helping because this week is his week off," Ben said.

"Ok then I will ask mine," replied Luke.

Dad said "Ok" and said that he would be there in a few moments he was just going to his shed to find some supplies. Ben then sprinted next door to get his dad and some pieces of timber.

Both fathers met at the end of the drive way and walked towards the children with unusual looks on their faces. They began to explain to us how they were going to build the tree house and afterwards would the children like to decorate it with paint? The children said "Yes" they would love to and in their tree house could they make a chalk board that could draw on?

The two fathers said, "Yes definitely, it is your tree house! Would you like to have it on the first on the second floor?" None of the children replied as it was a massive shock as the Dads said "The first or the second floor". This was above and beyond what the three expected.

They began building the tree house and eating the snacks that the mothers had been making in the kitchen. It was beginning to take shape. About three hours later the tree house was finished and was ready to be painted. Molly, Luke and Ben began to discuss their plans for the tree house. They all chose a side each to paint and went wild with the paint, it was flung from one side of the backyard to another! The parents were horrified when they came out with the next food course about how much mess the children had made! Although then they realised that it was only on the grass, it would wash off and, after all at least their children were having the time of their lives!!!

Adventure in Lolly Land

By Morgan Roe age 7. (Not entered in the competition)

The cow, the pig and the cat were searching for their ball. They looked high and low but couldn't find it. Then Cow said, "Hey, come over here, it might be in this wooden log."

They tried to see inside the log, but it was too dark. Then Cat said, "Hey, I'm the fastest of us all, so why don't I go back to our house to get the flashlight?"

And off he went. When he returned with the flashlight in his paws, they were able to see inside the log. But they still couldn't see the end of it. So they all went inside.

Finally they reached the end and in astonishment, there before them was a whole new world. They had a look around and then spotted a castle.

Pig said, "I wonder if there is any food in there."

Cow and Cat said, "Don't be silly. All you can think about now is your tummy."

Then Cow said, "Let's go inside and see what we can find."

Then they all marched through the door. The first room was super awesome. It was filled with lots of food and the King and Queens thrones.

Then a squeaky voice and a low, loud voice said, "Hi, hello. We're the King and Queen of Candy Land."

The Queen invited them to come over to their throne and share some cup cakes, lollies and a drink.

Pig said, "Sure, I want some of that."

So the three of them walked over to the throne.

Cat asked, "What is there to drink?"

The Queen replied, "We have magic butterfly milk, that turns into any flavour you want"

Then Pig asked, "Do you have any mud for me to splash in?"

The Queen said, "Not here, but if you go to the old farm, the pixie will offer you a mud bath."

Pig said, "Sure, how do I get there?"

Then the Queen said, "Quickly, go around the traffic lights that are run by pixie dust, then go over the old twisty bridge, over the candy floss mountain, and then you will arrive at the farm."

ThenCcow said, "Well we'll be off now to the farm."

But then the King and Queen said, "But aren't you forgetting something? We have a surprise for you. Wait a minute and we will go and get it for you."

In a flash the King and Queen came back. They said, "Here are your surprises."

They each received a basket of goodies for their journey to the farm. Then off they went to the farm. When they got to the traffic lights, a fairy shouted, "STOP! Are you new here?"

Cow said, "Yes we are new, and we are on our way to the farm." The fairy said, "You need to be careful when you go over the twisty bridge. I will give you each a bag of magic fairy dust to protect you."

So off they went on their way. Finally they got to the bridge, but couldn't see anything wrong. So they began to cross. When they were half way across, a dark shadow appeared. There before them was the Liquorice Man. He came towards them, and with every step, his shoes squeaked because they were made of liquorice.

Out of nowhere he said, "Why are you here?"

Pig said, "Because I want to have a mud bath at the farm. Are you made of real liquorice?

Then the Liquorice Man said, "Yes I am, why do you ask?"

"Because I love to eat liquorice."

The Liquorice Man said, "Oh no, I've never met anyone who wants to eat me before!"

Pig licked his lips and stared at him with hungry eyes. Then Pig walked slowly towards the Liquorice Man.

He cried, "Don't eat me I'm not as tasty as you think."

But Pig didn't stop and didn't say a word. Then the Liquorice Man ran away as fast as he could. As soon as he disappeared, the three of them crossed the bridge and headed towards Candy-floss Mountain. It was covered in fog and there were dark misty shadows. Then in the distance, was a big oak tree.

Cat said, "Yeh! Birds live in there."

Then Cat ran to the tree and peered upwards. Cat said, "Where are the birds?"

Cow said, "I don't know, but there in the tree was a little green animal."

Cat had never seen it before. It was a chameleon. Then the others recognised it too and said, "Hi there."

Cow said, "Hi, I'm Betty."

Pig said, "Hi, I'm food scraps."

And Cat said, "Hi, I'm Jimmy"

The chameleon said, "Hi, I'm Googly Eyes."

Cow said, "Is that because you have googly eyes?"

Googly Eyes said, "Yes, of course."

Then out of nowhere came a dark misty shadow. It was the Liquorice Man. He had a black wand in his hand.

He said, "Abracadabracadrip tree," and some liquorice came sprouting out of the wand.

Cat said, "Watch out guys!" and they all jumped behind a tree. Then the chameleon shouted, "gempo!"

Then out of nowhere flew a super hero. Her name was Flying Genius.

 She said, "Stop liquorice man, in the name of Candy Land!"

Liquorice Man said, "You'll never defeat me Flying Genius."

"Yes I will, I have new powers."

She cupped her hands and made a frosty cage, threw it at the Liquorice Man and he was trapped. Then Flying Genius told everyone to run away as fast as they could.

" My cage won't last forever. It's only made of ice as you know."

So they ran to a house made of leaves, petals and bricks. They knocked on the door.

A beautiful pixie said, "Hello, come inside."

So in they went. Then Pig asked the family of pixies, "You're not far from the candy floss mountain, are you?"

"No," said the pixies.

"You should run away with us, because the Liquorice Man is close."

The pixies said, "Sure."

And off they went. Soon they arrived at the farm. But they didn't know that the Liquorice Man had arrived before them. Unknown to them, the he had a flying contraption that helped him to travel faster than they could.

Pig said to a nice pixie behind the line up bench, "Is this where I get my ticket for the mud bath?"

"Yes," said the pixie. "Come with me and I'll take you to the mud bath."

So off they went. But Pig didn't realise that the nice pixie was really the Liquorice Man in disguise. And he led Pig to a mud bath. But instead of mud, it was filled with black, sticky liquorice with chocolate on top. Pig noticed that it smelt like liquorice.

He asked the nice pixie, "Why does this mud bath smell like liquorice?"

The pixie told a little lie. He said, "I don't know."

Pig said, "All right then, I'll just jump in to this lovely mud bath." Pig yelled, "Cannonball!"

He splashed into the nice mud. But it wasn't mud at all. He tried to get out, but he was stuck in this black, sticky liquorice.

The pixie giggled, and then took off his disguise and yelled, "I'm the Liquorice Man. You didn't recognise me. I fooled you. My plan worked. I'm going to have pork for dinner tonight."

Pig said, "But I didn't really want to eat you. I was just kiddin."

Liquorice Man said, "You may have been just kidding, but I still want to have you for dinner."

Meanwhile, Pig's friends Cat and Cow had realised that Pig had been missing for a long time. So they went to the mud bath entrance. There they asked a nice pixie, who had a note book in her hand, if she had the name food scraps written in her note book. The pixie said no.

Then Cow said, "All right, we'll have to look somewhere else."

But then Cat said to Cow, "Wasn't Pig carrying cup-cakes in his backpack to eat while he was here?"

Cow said, "Yes, and look, there is a trail of cup-cake crumbs."

Cat said, "We should follow it and then we might find Pig."

So they did, and there was Pig, stuck in a liquorice bath. The Liquorice Man was laughing at Pig.

Then the friends whispered, "Let's get our friends who live in the bubble gum tree, to bring some bubble gum fluff to stick on the Liquorice Man. That will weaken his powers."

So off they went to find them. Finally they found them, and together they took the bubble gum fluff and stuck it all over the Liquorice Man. When his powers were gone, Pig was able to escape from the liquorice bath which was no longer sticky. And then Pig, Cat and Cow all raced away back to the castle.

The Queen said, "There was a ball rolling through the town and we wondered who it belonged to. Two friendly giants said to the towns-people, why are you chasing that ball? The towns-people said, because we want to catch it and see if anyone comes looking for it. Then we can give it back to them."

Then Cat asked, "Was it a purple ball with orange spots?"

"Yes," said the Queen.

"Good," said Cat. "That's the ball we chased through the log and ended up here in Candy Land."

The Queen said, "We will take you to the giant's cloud and they will give you back your ball."

So off they went. Finally they reached the cloud, and Pig said, "How do we get up to the cloud?"

The Queen said, "We have to yell out to the giants and they will let down their magic ladder."

When the magic ladder came tumbling down, Pig, Cat, Cow and the Queen climbed up. When they got to the top, they knocked on the gigantic door. A big loud, echoing voice said, "Are you here for the ball?"

"Yes," said Cat.

"Here it is then. You can take it with you."

Then the Queen said, "Come with me back to the castle, and I will give you a present."

When they got to the castle the Queen said, "Wait here and I will go and get your presents."

When she returned she had three little baskets, one for Cat, one for Pig, and one for Cow. Inside they found lots and lots of stuffed toys and candy. The three friends picked up their baskets and their ball, and then all of the towns-people came into the castle and said, "Thank you for visiting Candy Land, and you must come again some time."

The Queen said, "Wait there and I will go and get the three magic crystals that will take you back to your world."

When she returned she gave them each a magic crystal, plus a magic locket so that they could come back anytime they wanted to. Pig, Cat and Cow then said, "Goooooooddddbbbbyyyeee everyone and thank you for everything you have done for us."

And then the magic crystals took them back to their land.

The End

A HOME FOR THE GNOME'S

By Charlotte Rumbal (3rd Adult)

Edward the Gnome is a humble wee chap

 with blue overalls and a baggy red hat.

He lives on a farm down a long country road

and an old pumpkin patch is his simple abode.

He doesn't do much for his job as a gnome,

he stands and he smiles in his pumpkin patch home.

But every year on the first day of fall

he makes his way down to the gnome annual ball.

The gnome annual ball is a special wee treat

with dancing and singing and good food to eat.

It happens at night at a quarter to one

and all gnomes are welcome to share in the fun.

But this year the ball was not like the rest,

for one thing the carrot cake wasn't the best.

For another, young Edward met a young lady

and when their eyes met his heart beat like crazy.

Her name was Wendy, she had a beautiful smile,

 long red hair, green eyes and a dress 'so in style'.

They danced all night under the light of the moon

 and when morning came it was over too soon.

So the two said goodbye but not forever

 and they met the next night which was awfully clever!

And the night after that and soon our friend Ed

and his lady friend Wendy met up to be wed.

After the wedding the bride and her gnome,

hitched a ride out of town to the countryside home.

They stood in the pumpkin patch under a leaf,

 Edward's smile so wide you could count all his teeth.

They stood and they looked at the grass and the trees

and the sheep in the paddocks all covered in fleece.

The world was so quiet, hardly ever a sound,

 which happens with not many people around.

And day after day they stood side by side,

 Edward the gnome and his beautiful bride.

But poor Wendy the gnome was not sharing the bliss,

 she thought of her home and her home she did miss.

Finally one night she had quite enough "I can't take it!"

she cried, "Life out here is too tough!

There's nothing to watch except a few sheep

and at night it's too quiet, I never can sleep."

"I'm going home," she said. "Where life is not dull!"

 Well Edward loved Wendy so he went as well.

To the city they went and took their gnome poses,

outside a large house in a garden of roses.

The garden looked out over a busy street,

 people rushed past all day in cars or on feet.

There was so much to see, to smell and to hear

 and the gnomes got attention for looking so dear.

A week soon passed in the gnome's new place,

Wendy's smile so big it took up her whole face.

But Edward was not the happiest gnome,

 he missed the farm and his pumpkin patch home.

One night he cried, "I have had quite enough!

 Life in the city is far far too tough."

It's so loud!" he said, "And the lights are too bright!

NO peace in the day and I can't sleep at night!"

Well our friends were in quite a pickle you see,

on where to call home they just couldn't agree.

For two days they argued over where they should stay,

 then for two days it was silent, with no more to say.

But then our friend Wendy had an idea.

"Let's leave," she said. "Let's get out of here,

let's go on a honeymoon, let's go today,

 and we'll work out our future while we're away."

In a bus baggage carrier the two hitched a ride

 on a bus that was heading for the seaside.

The drive took all day but at last they were there.

They climbed from the bus and breathed in the sea air.

Through a hedge ran the gnomes and they crept past a house,

 so silent they wouldn't have woken a mouse.

They crept across lawns at a slow steady pace,

looking and searching for just the right place.

Finally the gnomes came to a stop, they had found it!

At last! Their honeymoon spot.

They were outside a batch facing the sea,

in the shade of large Pohutakawa tree.

And as they began getting ready for bed,

the sun went down and turned the sea red.

"What a beautiful sight," Wendy said with a sigh,

and Edward agreed with his beautiful bride.

That night the waves lulled both gnomes to sleep,

noisy but calm like the soft baa of sheep,

and a light house nearby shone just enough light.

If only their homes could be like this at night!

The next day they talked about where to call home,

while watching the waves with their white frothy foam,

And enjoying the laughter of children nearby

and the cry of the seagulls flying past in the sky.

At last the day came for the gnomes to go home,

 but they still did not know to which home they should go.

To the farm or the city? Which would it be?

They both flopped to the ground in the shade of the tree.

And as they lay there trying to decide,

 it seemed that a message came from the seaside.

The waves crashing down on that warm sunny day

 all seemed to be whispering one word, "stay."

Edward jumped up so fast his hat fell from his head

and dancing with joy he excitedly said,

"Why Wendy the reason we could not agree

 is because we were meant to live here by the sea".

So Edward and Wendy decided to stay

 at the batch at the beach and they're still there today.

So if you're at the beach, look for the gnomes

 and compliment them on their wonderful home.

Side by side you will find them outside an old batch,

Ed in his overalls and baggy red hat,

and Wendy still wears her dress 'so in style'

and both gnomes are smiling gigantic big smiles.

Zoë and Zebedee's Zoo Safari

Illustrated and written by Alex Stone (2nd Adult)

Little Zoë Stone and her brother Zebedee went to the zoo one day with their Dad, who is a poet.

Like most poets, he is a *struggling* poet, and does other writing to pay the bills.

But mostly, Zoë and Zebedee's Mum pays the bills.

Anyway, they had a grand old time at the zoo, especially when Dad made up rhymes for some of the animals.

Zoë, who is only four, didn't understand some of the words, but she loves the sound of her Dad's voice when he is happy, and especially when he is reciting poems. *Especially* poems about animals.

Zebedee is nine years old. He was born in Africa, and remembers seeing big animals on the *veld* there. His cousin, Natasha, lives on a real game reserve, with real elephants, real lions, real kudu. One time, Natasha was late for school - their bus had been held up by lions!

Zebedee told Zoë to imagine they were going on a *safari*, to visit all the animals of the world. A *poetic zoo safari*.

That was totally cool with Zoë, who's right into adventures - any kind!

Zebedee likes facts. His favourite book is his big colour encyclopedia.

So, on their zoo safari, Zebedee's Dad also told them interesting things about each animal. He called it Zoo Trivia. He also said it was all true.

Stuff that not many people would know about. Stuff in his poems. Stuff that wasn't on the little old signs at the zoo...

Giraffa camelopardalis ....read the first sign.

"See these long words?" said Zoë and Zeb's Dad. "That's the proper, scientific name for giraffes. I'll explain why all animals need two names."

He paused. Then he smiled. Then he took up his poet's stance. "Uh, oh," thought Zebedee to himself, "He's going to embarrass us." And sure enough, he did - well sort of, because Z & Z were kinda proud too.

Zebedee and Zoë's Dad puffed his chest, spread his arms wide, and lit up his eyes. And then, using his best rumbly voice, he said -

Spotted camels?

Get real Linnaeus -

if we weren't gentle

we'd get mental

at what you tried to call us!

"Carolus Linnaeus was a Swedish scientist who worked in the 1700's. He started the system of classifying all the plants and creatures of the world into genus and species," he continued, "*Giraffa* is the genus; *camelopardis* the species.

Genus is the *family* the animal belongs to. The species is all the animals that are *the same*: they live in the similar places, have the same habits, and can breed together.

Giving all animals a double name like this makes sure we don't confuse them with each other. So far, it's proved to be a workable way of classifying all the species of the world.

If you were a giraffe, would you be happy being described as a kind of camel-leopard? Dunno if I would…

Anyway, here's the giraffe poem," and he puffed himself up again: saying....

Giraffes - supermodels of the veld.

Blue-black and beautiful

in its penthouse in the sky

the tongue of the giraffe enjoys a penthouse view

from animalia's topmost pew.

and Zounds!

they do make sounds,

but on occasions rare and few.

They can moo, they can bleat,

they can bellow, bull-like too.

They can grunt, cough, tweet and growl,

but we at this here zoo

have never ever heard them howl.

And if they snore (as they sometimes do)

catch it quick! For they sleep

upon their feet

in brief two minute bits.

Leggy, graceful, stylishly swept

*with **ossicones** upon their heads*

and dapple patterned, groovy threads;

Plus!Eyes and lashes made to melt,

you could call these

the supermodels of the veld.

Zoë laughed and clapped her hands, and danced a little jig.

"How about some Zoo Trivia?" asked her Dad.

"Yeah OK," said Zebedee. "But quietly."

"Giraffes have majorly high blood pressure," Dad informed them.

"Their huge hearts need to pump 75 litres of blood every minute with enough power to reach their brains 5m above the ground.

So they can't lie down. Their heads couldn't stand the pressure. "

"You mean their heads might explode?" asked Zebedee incredulously.

"Sort of," said their Dad.

Down this way, looming large,

(said their Dad),

come see the elephants

- no extra charge!

"Let's skip!" said Zoë.

"Get real," said Zebedee.

"Stop!" said their Dad, "Check this out! Here's a hedgehog walking along the path. She doesn't need a special enclosure - this whole park counts as her *natural habitat*. That's the name for the place where you can comfortably live. And nobody would want to eat her. So she has no natural enemies, here, too."

While the children looked at the hedgehog, Dad stood and mused.

".....actually, this is not *really* hedgehog habitat. They were brought here from England, but that's a long story. Tell you later. C'mon, where are those elephants?"

But on the way, they found -

Grey Headed Fruit Bat

(*Pteropus poliocephalus*)

Imagine flying!

I'm sure that you have -

its every human's genes.

Imagine more:

threading through the dark

following your screams.

Echolocation - call it natural inspiration

for radar

and blockbusters,

and comic book machines.

Its the stuff of superheroes

the Batman in our dreams.

Imagine flying!

Fingers stroking you in flight

Imagine flying!

I reckon it would be alright

Imagine flying!

Bats do it every night!

"Here are some 'Batfacts' for you, Zeb," said his Dad. "And we'll debunk some 'Batmyths' at the same time."

Blind as a bat? No way: all bat species can see, most of them extremely well. And in the dark too!

Bats in your hair? Get real: do you think an animal with state-of-the-art echolocation navigation systems would blunder into your beehive? Would they *want* to?

Flying rats? Wrong again: bats are not rodents. Bats are actually more closely related to humans than to rats and mice.

Airborne bumblers? *Nyet*: unlike most birds, bats can fly at low speed with extreme manoeuverability. It's control all the way!

Blood-sucking monsters? Half truth: most of the 900 bat species eat insects; a number are vegetarians; some eat flowers, or sip nectar; one type catches fish; a few eat anything; and oh, yes, there are a few species in Central America which live on the blood of animals. There are no vampire bats in Europe - nowhere near Dracula's castle.

Zebedee had gone on to the next enclosure. "Check out these big billy goats!" he called, and Zoë came running. Dad followed, more dignified.

Barbary Sheep - mountain machos.

(*Ammotragus lervia*)

A wild horned sheep from the Atlas Mountains in North Africa, also known as the Aoudad, said the small zoo sign.

Dad said, instead:

If sheep can be macho,

that is what we are:

the Rambos of the order Caprinae

running wild on the

lofty Atlas hills

in the wilds of Tunisia.

But, we're running hunted

used for meat, hides, skin and sinew

and unlike our mate Rambo

we got horns, not guns, to blambo

back at the humans who make our numbers few,

and fewer every year.

Zoë's Dad saw that her attention was wandering, so he spun her a little teaser:

Legend has it zebra's greedy

but come and see -

and you'll agree

at least his coat's not seedy!

Zoe's Dad winked at her, and she ran on ahead to the next enclosure.

Zebras - mobile Op Art

(Equus quagga bohmi)

Kwa-ha-ha

goes a zebra's bark

and that's just one of the things that make us smart.

See this coat, this dazzling pelt?

It's the mobile Op Art of the veld:

we're flashing past, in groups of friends

tell me where one zebra ends!

Stripes, they do have uses other -

like babies wanting to find mother

each of us is unique you see

our stripes mark us fingerprintedly!

Dapper, dashing bold and bright

we'd label us a splendid sight.

What are we? said the zoo sign,

(Pictures showed Grant's, Grevy's and Hartmann's zebra patterns.)

Yes, you're right! We are Grant's zebra.

Zoë heard Zebedee reading the sign. "What are we?" she repeated, and asked her Dad.

He thought for a while. He said, "Yeah, good question, Liddle Ziddle." (That was what he sometimes called her). "We should have our own sign at the zoo. We're animals too."

Consider yourself....

(*Homo sapiens sapiens*)

Human, zooman

Yes, that's you!

Amanda, Bill, Cassie and Dan

Zeb and Zoë, and you and you,

are all here living in a zoo.

You see, we humans are part of creation

but somehow, we've lost sight of our rightful station:

we're animals (mammals to be exact)

too successful for ourselves - that's a fact.

Distributed worldwide, we live almost everywhere

and deny other species of their fair share.

We're part of nature, to be sure....

but - and it's the biggest kid of but -

we're far more dangerous than before:

*We can build, walk, talk and **destroy**:*

Fellow Homo sapiens sapiens,

Human, zooman

let's not treat our planet as a toy!

And he added,

Consider yourself...part of the family,

Consider yourself...one of us!

"Ok, Dad," said Zebedee, "so I'm also a mammal. But look how different I am to this camel!"

"It's called diversity," said his Dad. "Mammals are different because they evolved to be good at different things. Take this camel now: she may look strange, but she's totally OK in the desert. Camels can survive in places where we can't."

...and he was off again!

A Technogeeks Dream Machine

(Camelus dromedarius - Arabian camel)

If a camel was a car

the model would go far.

If a camel was a car

it sure would win

from Paris to Daka.

Rally-bred tried and true -

packed with many extras

(to make non-owners vextrous)

and with vices small and few.

Fuel efficiency

is the special key:

which you could say, was ironic

though arguably moronic

since mates,

they come from Gulf-side oil-rich states!

A copywriter's dream

this camel-wamel car,

a technogeek's machine

with a triple wipers on the screen

and big fat tackies for the tar;

much, much more than just

a simple-wimple dune buggy

It leaves the others in the dust!

Now put this in the mix-

It's built to carry six

without much extra effort

(but, says a voice in the back

"It's a dubious sort of comfort,

like being on a rack")

If a camel was a car

the model would go far!

If a camel was a car

from Paris to Dakar!

Anti-theft aesthetics

Camels are ugly. And they spit.

 (said some graffiti on the zoo sign)

"What's aesthetics?" asked Zoë.

"Dunno," said Zebedee.

"It means how things look," said Dad.

We're trained professionals. Don't try this at home!

Camels can go for up to *six months without drinking!*

When we finally find water, we suck *135 litres in less than six minutes!* (said the real sign)

"Wow!" said Zebedee, incredulously. (That's what his Dad lives for - to impress the kids)

But Zoë was already skipping away. "Hey Dad, come look at this big thing in the water!" she yelled.

Amazing amphibians

(Hippopotamus amphibius)

Exercise? Schmexercise!

all I do is eat:

a hippo's life

is hardly strife,

cooling heels, out

of the midday heat.

I'm downright cool, within this pool

in these here murky depths.

And with this kind of laughing gear,

who do I have to fear?

Saving energy is my forte

and that's what I do all day.

I'm waiting for the stars to shimmer

before I go for dinner.

Trouble is, all I eat is salads-

So how come it is

I weigh as much as Harrods?

By now, Zebedee and Zoë were tired; Dad was tired; time to head on home.

In the car, Zebedee said dreamily, "I wish we had a book of all the animals in the zoo..."

"Yeah!" enthused Zoë. "One with all the poems Dad made!"

"Well, let's see what we can do," said their Dad, with a secret smile....

Children's fiction available from Rangitawa Publishing

Milly Feather
Childrenz One
Childrenz Two